Dear Parent:

Your child's love of reading starts here!

Every child learns to read in a different way and at his or her own speed. Some go back and forth between reading levels and read favorite books again and again. Others read through each level in order. You can help your young reader improve and become more confident by encouraging his or her own interests and abilities. From books your child reads with you to the first books he or she reads alone, there are I Can Read Books for every stage of reading:

SHARED READING
Basic language, word repetition, and whimsical illustrations, ideal for sharing with your emergent reader

BEGINNING READING
Short sentences, familiar words, and simple concepts for children eager to read on their own

READING WITH HELP
Engaging stories, longer sentences, and language play for developing readers

READING ALONE
Complex plots, challenging vocabulary, and high-interest topics for the independent reader

I Can Read Books have introduced children to the joy of reading since 1957. Featuring award-winning authors and illustrators and a fabulous cast of beloved characters, I Can Read Books set the standard for beginning readers.

A lifetime of discovery begins with the magical words "I Can Read!"

Visit www.icanread.com for information
on enriching your child's reading experience.

ISBN 978-0-06-301707-8

20 21 22 23 24 LSCC 10 9 8 7 6 5 4 3 2 1 ❖ First Edition

It's Showtime!

by Colin Hosten

Based on the Screenplay by Mike White

Produced by Allison Shearmur, Angelina Jolie,
Brigham Taylor

Directed by Thea Sharrock

HARPER

An Imprint of HarperCollinsPublishers

Hi, I'm Ivan.

I'm a silverback gorilla.

Welcome to my home!

We have the best circus in town.

I am the star of the show.

My friends are in the show, too.

Frankie loves his ball, and Murphy

loves his firetruck.

Henrietta and Thelma both love

to laugh.

Bob is one of my best friends.

He's not in the show.

But he likes to hang around anyway.

Stella is my other best friend.

She's also in the show.

Stella has a big part.

The circus is in the Big Top Mall.

The mall has many stores.

This brings people to the mall!

My friend Mack runs the show.

He calls me the One and Only Ivan.

This is my friend Julia.

She likes to draw.

I wish I could draw as good as Julia.

I have many talents.

I can let out a big roar!

People don't want to see me roar.

Mack wishes I could do more.

Maybe I should switch to drawing.

Julia thinks I'm good at it.

One day, a new star joins the show.

Her name is Ruby.

Everybody loves her.

I think they love Ruby more than me!

But at least the show is popular.

Oh, no!

Stella isn't feeling well.

She can't be in the show anymore.

Now Ruby is scared to perform.

She is too nervous without Stella.

I want to help Ruby feel better.

Maybe a drawing will cheer her up.

That gives the circus an idea!

Everybody comes to see me draw.

I am the star of the show again!

Ruby is still sad.

She wants to go home.

My friends and I leave the circus!

Uh-oh!

This isn't the jungle!

We return back to the circus.

I paint a picture for Ruby.

It is the jungle where I was born.

Ruby loves my painting!

Julia also loves my painting.

She tells everybody about it.

Now everyone is talking about me.

They want to help me and my friends.

They ask Mack to let us go home.

He wants us to do more shows.

But the people protest.

They make signs to free us.

Finally, Mack has to close the show.

My friends and I can go home now!

I will miss everyone.

But I will miss Mack most of all.

I like it here in my new home.

It looks just like my painting.

There are lots of trees to climb.

Ruby loves her new home, too.

She makes lots of new friends.

They love her very much.

I am glad I helped Ruby go home.

I loved being the One and Only Ivan.

But now I can finally relax.